Other titles available:

Blue Saves the Day

Doug the Busy Digger

Fairy Sunshine

Rags the Brave Puppy

The Troublesome Twins

ISBN 1-84135-235-7 (cased)
ISBN 1-84135-252-7 (limp)

Copyright © 2003 Award Publications Limited

First published 2003

Published by Award Publications Limited,
27 Longford Street, London NW1 3DZ

Printed in Malaysia

Patty Pig
Gets a Job

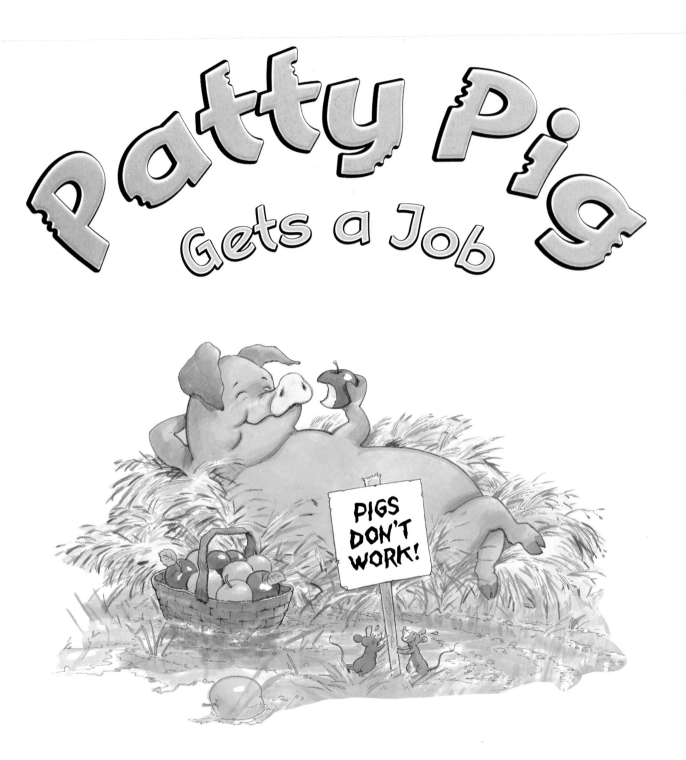

PIGS DON'T WORK!

Written by Lesley Rees
Illustrated by Gary Rees

AWARD PUBLICATIONS LIMITED

Every animal on Sunnyside Farm has an important job to do.

MOO-MOO! MOO-MOO! The cows supply tasty, creamy milk for the farmer's children to drink.

CLIP-CLOP! CLIP-CLOP!

The horse pulls the cart that takes
the farmer's wife to market.

CLUCK-CLUCK! CLUCK-CLUCK!
The hens lay lots of speckled
eggs for the family's breakfast.

BAA-BAA! BAA-BAA! The cuddly sheep give up their fleeces to make soft, warm wool, which the farmer's wife knits into nice warm jumpers.

BAA-BAA!

BAA-BAA!

All the animals are kept very busy. All except one – Patty Pig.

All day long, Patty lies in her sty, wallowing, eating and snoozing. She doesn't see why she should do anything to help around the farm and doesn't care what the other animals think.

"My job is wallowing, eating and snoozing,"
she grunts. "And I'm very good at it."

But the other animals aren't happy. It really isn't fair. Patty has such an easy life.

"Let's find her a job!" neighs Henry Horse.

And all the other animals agree.

"But I've got a job," snorts Patty.
"Wallowing, eating and snoozing!"

The animals take no notice. "Come on!" they cry.
"Let's find you something useful to do."

"Okay, okay," she oinks. "I'm coming. But I CAN'T give milk...

... and I DON'T lay eggs!

So what CAN I do?"

"You can pull my cart," says Henry, popping the harness over Patty's head. "Come on, off you trot."

But it isn't very long before it all goes wrong. WIBBLE-WOBBLE-WIBBLE-

BANG!

Poor Patty can't trot fast enough and the cart keeps banging her big pink bottom.

"OWWW!" she cries. "Please give me something else to try."

QUACK!

"I know," miaows Chivers Cat, "you can help me catch mice in the barn."

But those naughty, scampering mice just run round and round, until Patty is so dizzy, she collapses in a heap!

"Never mind," woofs Shep Sheepdog.
"Come and help me round up the sheep."
"Okay," grumbles Patty, "but I don't
think I'll be any good at it."

And she's right. When she trots into the field, the sheep stand very, very still and just laugh and laugh. Patty feels very silly!

"See!" she snorts, grumpily. "I told you. There's nothing I can do! I'm going back to my sty for a snack and a snooze. I don't want to be disturbed."

So Patty waddles back through the farmyard towards her sty, completely unaware that she's being followed.

All the baby animals on the farm are flapping, trotting, wobbling and waddling behind Patty.

PIGS DON'T WORK!

The little animals see how warm and cuddly Patty looks, and think she's just right to snuggle up to!

Patty settles in the straw for a nap.
Quickly, the babies flap, trot and wobble
into her sty and snuggle against her.

Patty is very surprised, but she doesn't mind and gives them all a big cuddle. In no time at all, everyone is fast asleep and snoring — ZZZzzzz.

When the mummies and daddies stop work for the day, they can't believe their eyes. Patty has found the perfect job after all. She's the farm's very own babysitter!

Now, when all the animals are working, Patty is working too, looking after all the babies on Sunnyside Farm.

PATTY PIG'S PLAY GROUP